A Place No Flowers Grow

Books by Cheryl Cantafio

MY STAY WITH THE SISTERS: POEMS

BARRY AND THE BIG JUMP
(November 2024)

for Tito

Copyright © 2024 by Cheryl Cantafio

All rights reserved. No part of this book may be used or reproduced in any manner whatsoever without written permission from the author except in the case of brief quotations embodied in critical articles and reviews.

This is a work of fiction. Names, characters, businesses, places, events, locales, and incidents are either the products of the author's imagination or used in a fictitious manner. Any resemblance to actual persons, living or dead, or actual events is purely coincidental.

Editor: Shelby Leigh
Copy Editors: Ariane Peveto and Jackie Peveto
Cover and Book Design: Islam Farid

ISBN: 979-8-9880452-2-9 (paperback)

First edition 2024
Printed in the United States

Contents

11	*Part I* **and so we begin**	
12	legend of the vale	
13	Octavia	
14	Roen	
15	Fox	
16	Alyeska	
17	devil's nettle	
18	last wish	
19	bait and switch	
20	worlds colliding	
23	*Part II* **love blooms**	
24	new beginning	
25	chasing dreams	
26	no sunset	
27	Roen's folly	
28	first impressions	
29	thunderstruck i	
30	jumping into the deep end	
31	tell me about yourself i	
32	tell me about yourself ii	
33	wildflowers	
34	revelation	
35	revontulet	
36	lovely weirdos	
37	home i	
38	home ii	
39	betrothed	
40	the road ahead	

41 *Part III*
scientific curiosities

42 prisoner
43 scamp
44 experiment i
45 fury
46 experiment ii
47 vixen
48 observation
49 miscalculation
50 hypothesis i
51 hypothesis ii
52 experiment iii
53 outcome
54 unshackled
55 unknown variable
56 victory meal
57 exile
58 rest

59 *Part IV*
marriage in the making

60 the location
61 stranger danger
62 setting the stage
63 save the date
64 something old
65 something new
66 something red
67 something's askew
68 premonition
69 honeymoon plans
70 rehearsal dinner
71 in memoriam
72 kiss me good night

	Part V
73	**'til death parts us**
74	flowers for the bride
75	pocket bouquet
76	superstitious
77	minus one
78	ladies in waiting
79	a race to the first
80	hesitant
81	first look photos
82	ceremony
83	thunderstruck ii
84	woman scorned
85	bubbly
86	crimson vows
87	seven minutes
88	procession
89	shattered
90	reception
91	eulogy
92	haunted widow/haunted life
93	**Epilogue**
94	three years later
95	Octavia's folly
96	reunited
97	whispers of the vale
99	acknowledgments
100	about the poem formats
101	about the author
102	about the editors and book cover designer

A Place No Flowers Grow

a poetic tale by

Cheryl Cantafio

Be aware of content warnings and take care of potential triggers: animal medical experimentation, biting/blood, graphic death, death of a loved one, gore, grief, and violence.

Part I
and so we begin

legend of the vale

among the blue ice caves and foxglove
there lies a shadowy tale
two people madly in love
their story part of the glacial vale

there lies a shadowy tale
a bride in an ivory sequined dress
their story part of the glacial vale
a groom waiting to say yes

a bride in an ivory sequined dress
to have and to hold
a groom waiting to say yes
fates sealed with rings of gold

to have and to hold
two people madly in love
fates sealed with rings of gold
among the blue ice caves and foxglove

Octavia

a woman once lived here
emerald eyes and bright smile
born on the last frontier
raised along the arctic mile

emerald eyes and bright smile
entranced by fireweed and forget-me-nots
raised along the arctic mile
danced among her momma's flowerpots

entranced by fireweed and forget-me-nots
mindful of Bear and Caribou and Fox
danced among her momma's flowerpots
bold and smart and curious

mindful of Bear and Caribou and Fox
born on the last frontier
bold and smart and curious
there once lived a woman named Octavia

Roen

a man once lived elsewhere
he had dark and kindly eyes
longing for adventure and fresh air
looking for his opportunity to rise

he had dark and kindly eyes
impatient with academia and theory
looking for his opportunity to rise
drawn to something extraordinary

impatient with academia and theory
he needed variation
drawn to something extraordinary
for meteoric discoveries and innovation

he needed variation
longing for adventure and fresh air
for meteoric discoveries and innovation
there once lived a man named Roen

Fox

there once lived an arctic queen
Fox, indigo-eyed and full of cheer
thriving, inquisitive, and keen
in the snowbanks of the last frontier

Fox, indigo-eyed and full of cheer
a huntress alert and aware
in the snowbanks of the last frontier
she had a family under her care

a huntress alert and aware
Fox looked for eggs to steal
she had a family under her care
listened for her next meal

Fox looked for eggs to steal
thriving, inquisitive, and keen
listened for her next meal
there once lived a queen named Fox

Alyeska

north to the future is what they call it
it's beautiful and brutal
glaciers, wintergreens, and grit
people and animals rootle

it's beautiful and brutal
exposed in the midnight sun
people and animals rootle
under the stealth of polar nights

exposed in the midnight sun
where the water is crystal clear
under the stealth of polar nights
people and animals discover their last frontier

where the water is crystal clear
glaciers, wintergreens, and grit
people and animals discover their last frontier
north to the future is what they call it

devil's nettle

Octavia befriended the devil's nettle
at an early age
yarrow filled her momma's kettle
along with chamomile and sage

at an early age
her momma collected herbs
along with chamomile and sage
for all that ails and disturbs

her momma collected herbs
it relieved her sorrows and put her at ease
for all that ails and disturbs
but Momma's teas couldn't cure her own disease

it relieved her sorrows and put her at ease
yarrow filled her momma's kettle
but Momma's teas couldn't cure her own disease
not even with devil's nettle

last wish

live, my dear boy, live
Roen's grandfather signed to him
run, my dear boy, run
find your own rhythm

Roen's grandfather signed to him
it wouldn't be much longer
find your own rhythm
Roen tried to be stronger

it wouldn't be much longer
Grandfather closed his eyes
Roen tried to be stronger
promised his grandfather he'd try

Grandfather closed his eyes
run, my dear boy, run
promised his grandfather he'd try
live, my dear boy, live

bait and switch

pounce, pounce, pounce!
Fox prepares for the upcoming week
forages for every meaty ounce
listens for a prey's chirp or squeak

Fox prepares for the upcoming week
devouring a lemming here and there
listens for a prey's chirp or squeak
her mate almost catches a hare

devouring a lemming here and there
Fox must snatch meals for her kit
her mate almost catches a hare
captivated by a smell before she quit

Fox must snatch meals for her kit
forages for every meaty ounce
captivated by a smell before she quit
pounce, pounce, snap!

worlds colliding

life altering
somewhere magical
Alyeska
i want to go there

somewhere magical
scientific discoveries
i want to go there
endless possibilities

scientific discoveries
natural medicines
endless possibilities
it's all right here

natural medicines
survival of the fittest
it's all right here
civil, wild, intoxicating

survival of the fittest
they sense something wonderful
civil, wild, intoxicating
what's over there?

they sense something wonderful
it's magnetic
what's over there?
it's calling them

it's magnetic
it's the push, the pull
it's calling them
it's their destinies

it's the push, the pull
Alyeska
it's their destinies
life altering

Part II
love blooms

new beginning

Roen arrived in his grandfather's coat
beginning a new chapter in his story
a polar paradise by air or by boat
a shiny new laboratory

beginning a new chapter in his story
he shivered in anticipation
a shiny new laboratory
a white fox broke his concentration

he shivered in anticipation
the glacial setting suited him just fine
a white fox broke his concentration
the cold beauty of it all was divine

the glacial setting suited him just fine
a polar paradise by air or by boat
the cold beauty of it all was divine
Roen arrived in his grandfather's coat

chasing dreams

Octavia's so happy she could burst
she's got an optimistic spirit
tantalizingly immersed
at the epicenter of it

she's got an optimistic spirit
full of high hopes and anticipation
at the epicenter of it
at the hub of experimentation

full of high hopes and anticipation
working in an agro-science lab
at the hub of experimentation
with people who love to confab

working in an agro-science lab
tantalizingly immersed
with people who love to confab
Octavia's so happy she could burst

no sunset

the never-ending light—in it creeps
how does anyone discern day from night?
Roen needs to get some sleep
his curtains aren't putting up much of a fight

how does anyone discern day from night?
Octavia is awake and feels so alive
his curtains aren't putting up much of a fight
the vegetables in her garden thrive

Octavia is awake and feels so alive
she adores her early morning stroll
the vegetables in her garden thrive
the midnight sun warms Octavia's soul

she adores her early morning stroll
Roen needs to get some sleep
the midnight sun warms Octavia's soul
the never-ending light—in it creeps

Roen's folly

Roen wonders why he took this job
in the middle of nowhere
the cold makes his hands throb
the snowy winds ruffle his hair

in the middle of nowhere
no one hears the animals scream
the snowy winds ruffle his hair
his ambition and resolve guiltily stream

no one hears the animals scream
it's for science, though, right?
his ambition and resolve guiltily stream
his mettle tested by the never-ending white

it's for science, though, right?
the cold makes his hands throb
his mettle tested by the never-ending white
Roen wonders why he took this job

first impressions

Roen found a joyful place
the local greasy spoon would be fun
right time, right space
after the workday was done

the local greasy spoon would be fun
Octavia needed a break
after the workday was done
she went for a bite and a milkshake

Octavia needed a break
Roen tucked into his beer
she went for a bite and a milkshake
her laugh gave him welcome cheer

Roen tucked into his beer
right time, right space
her laugh gave him welcome cheer
Roen found a joyful place

thunderstruck i

Roen was thunderstruck by her
the charge of a new endeavor
he felt his cold heart stir
she would be his forever

the charge of a new endeavor
he felt something inside him shatter
she would be his forever
if only he was brave enough to ask her

he felt something inside him shatter
he felt his lonely world sway
if only he was brave enough to ask her
and then Octavia looked his way

he felt his lonely world sway
he felt his cold heart stir
and then Octavia looked his way
Roen was thunderstruck by her

jumping into the deep end

why now? why not now?
Octavia's outside voice betrayed her
i just said yes—holy cow
butterflies in her stomach started to stir

Octavia's outside voice betrayed her
i can't believe i said yes
butterflies in her stomach started to stir
do i have to wear a dress?

i can't believe i said yes
i can't believe she said yes
do i have to wear a dress?
Roen looked like a nervous mess

i can't believe she said yes
i just said yes—holy cow
Roen looked like a nervous mess
why now? why not now?

tell me about yourself i

Octavia opened up to him
an extrovert since birth
she followed both her passion and whim
used her hands to play in the earth

an extrovert since birth
Momma taught her horticulture and science
used her hands to play in the earth
Papa taught her tenacity and self-reliance

Momma taught her horticulture and science
she studied sustainability and agro
Papa taught her tenacity and self-reliance
to make crops thrive where they should not grow

she studied sustainability and agro
she followed both her passion and whim
to make crops thrive where they should not grow
Octavia opened up to him

tell me about yourself ii

Roen opened up to her
he was a quiet child by choice
like Grandfather, an inquisitive entrepreneur
he scared Mum when he (loudly) found his voice

he was a quiet child by choice
Mum and Grandfather used their hands to talk
he scared Mum when he (loudly) found his voice
he could sign before he could walk

Mum and Grandfather used their hands to talk
he studied the structure of the arctic fox's ear
he could sign before he could walk
to create natural tech so others could hear

he studied the structure of the arctic fox's ear
like Grandfather, an inquisitive entrepreneur
to create natural tech so others could hear
Roen opened up to her

wildflowers

Roen gave a bouquet of wildflowers to her
Octavia's momma taught her all about them
memories inside her started to stir
the yarrow tea made from petal and stem

Octavia's momma taught her all about them
Roen's grandfather taught him about buttercups
the yarrow tea made from petal and stem
skin glowed from holding them close up

Roen's grandfather taught him about buttercups
she spoke about flowers that bloom in low light
skin glowed from holding them close up
he would always remember this night

she spoke about flowers that bloom in low light
memories inside her started to stir
he would always remember this night
he wanted to give all the wildflowers to her

revelation

Octavia's on to something
Alyeska's wildflowers held the key
she felt inspiration spring
unable to contain her glee

Alyeska's wildflowers held the key
she scribbled down her notes
unable to contain her glee
this was the antidote

she scribbled down her notes
a puzzle unlocked
this was the antidote
it would take time to concoct

a puzzle unlocked
she felt inspiration spring
it would take time to concoct
Octavia's on to something

revontulet

fox fires
revontulet
blues and greens and ambers
stars sprayed across the sky to light
their kiss

lovely weirdos

we make lovely weirdos
she had freakish upper body strength
he made hand puppets in the shadows
they laughed about their quirks at length

she had freakish upper body strength
Papa taught me how to defend myself
they laughed about their quirks at length
you're strong for a tiny elf

Papa taught me how to defend myself
she was defenseless in her love for him
you're strong for a tiny elf
she made him feel weak in every limb

she was defenseless in her love for him
he made hand puppets in the shadows
she made him feel weak in every limb
we could make lovely little weirdos

home i

it feels like home
when Roen embraces Octavia
when he writes silly little love notes
she feels whole in his presence

when Roen embraces Octavia
all of her loneliness melts away
she feels whole in his presence
like she could conquer the world

all of her loneliness melts away
his confidence in her is foreplay
like she could conquer the world
her heart soars

his confidence in her is foreplay
when he writes silly little love notes
her heart soars
it feels like home

home ii

this is home
Alyeska
Roen seems himself here
with Octavia

Alyeska
midnight sun and cold as hell
with Octavia
paradise found, and it's heavenly

midnight sun and cold as hell
he loves her
paradise found, and it's heavenly
he is overjoyed

he loves her
Roen seems himself here
he is overjoyed
this is home

betrothed

the ring
symbolizes
generations of love
shimmering in art deco and
sapphires

the road ahead

what does the future hold?
so many places to find love
adventures so bright, so bold
among the forget-me-not and foxglove

so many places to find love
who would have thought it was here?
among the forget-me-not and foxglove
partners in love and career

who would have thought it was here?
their hearts are exploding
partners in love and career
and an unshakeable foreboding

their hearts are exploding
adventures so bright, so bold
and an unshakeable foreboding
what does the future hold?

Part III
scientific curiosities

prisoner

Fox is no longer free
her fur has started to shed
she is desperate to flee
they lured her with the freshly dead

her fur has started to shed
the view is gray and desolate
they lured her with the freshly dead
she's unwell in the metal crate

the view is gray and desolate
the cage floor stabs at her feet
she's unwell in the metal crate
the food barely tastes like meat

the cage floor stabs at her feet
she is desperate to flee
the food barely tastes like meat
Fox needs to be free

scamp

the fox
this feral beast
is a doppelganger
of the dog he rescued as
a boy

experiment i

Roen taught Fox simple commands
Fox glared at him through her cage
she wasn't in a position to yowl demands
she yelped her outrage

Fox glared at him through her cage
he threw her an extra treat
she yelped her outrage
how eager she was to eat

he threw her an extra treat
Fox felt a great deal of distress
how eager she was to eat
he was quite pleased with her progress

Fox felt a great deal of distress
she wasn't in a position to yowl demands
he was quite pleased with her progress
Roen taught Fox simple commands

fury

this fool
continues to
poke and prod and test Fox
she is imprisoned; her fury
festers

experiment ii

Fox had grown (her powers too)
Roen placed her on a new protocol
Fox learned things that were brand-new
she was insulted by his gall

Roen placed her on a new protocol
Fox missed the thrill of the hunt
she was insulted by his gall
Fox heard lemmings chatter and bears grunt

Fox missed the thrill of the hunt
she reached her limit with this test
Fox heard lemmings chatter and bears grunt
Fox bit him, drew blood in protest

she reached her limit with this test
Fox learned things that were brand-new
Fox bit him, drew blood in protest
Fox had grown (her powers too)

vixen

tell me about your other woman
Octavia said in jest
you mean my wintry noblewoman?
she's quite the conquest

Octavia said in jest
Roen told her about his arctic fox
she's quite the conquest
Fox glared at them behind the locks

Roen told her about his arctic fox
Fox could keenly hear and smell
Fox glared at them behind the locks
her intelligence and fury started to swell

Fox could keenly hear and smell
you mean my wintry noblewoman?
her intelligence and fury started to swell
Fox could hear him tell the woman

observation

Fox watched them from her box
her entrapment will be short-lived
they took note of Fox
Fox wondered if her own mate still lived

her entrapment will be short-lived
the fool gently nuzzled his mate
Fox wondered if her own mate still lived
he guided her to Fox's crate

the fool gently nuzzled his mate
the fool's mate called Fox a striking *wolf*
he guided her to Fox's crate
the fool looked stunned and weary

the fool's mate called Fox *a striking wolf*
they took note of Fox
the fool looked stunned and weary
Fox watched them from her box

miscalculation

your fox
is not a fox,
Octavia whispered,
you can't release her. Roen frowned
I know

hypothesis i

Fox felt different
was her revenge possible?
too large for her entrapment
she could be unstoppable

was her revenge possible?
she couldn't take it much longer
she could be unstoppable
that fool had made her stronger

she couldn't take it much longer
Fox knew her growth was an equalizer
that fool had made her stronger
and he was none the wiser

Fox knew her growth was an equalizer
too large for her entrapment
and he was none the wiser
Fox felt different

hypothesis ii

could Fox
get the fool to
understand she is not
property? she is not *Dog*; she
is *Fox*

tonight
Fox would attempt
the fool's language with words
she learned. Fox yelped *SIT*, and cellmates
complied

Fox thought
they are not *Dog*
they are Alyeska's beasts
Fox would free them, too. *Patience, beasts*
patience

experiment iii

Roen
pulled Fox from her
enclosure; she growled *NO*
astonished, he clamored to take
control

outcome

they say
things sprout bigger
during the midnight sun
Fox saw her escape, took it, and
broke free

unshackled

Fox knew
the fool placed a
metal object inside
her—she liberated it and
herself

unknown variable

vanished
Roen betrayed
his progress a distant
memory, a factor erased
by snow

victory meal

the call of prey is so strong
Fox is ravenous for the hunt
those rapid heartbeats a tempting song
Fox races to the polar front

Fox is ravenous for the hunt
she would give her prey a fright
Fox races to the polar front
Fox will feast well tonight

she would give her prey a fright
sweet meats, sweet blood, no sharing
Fox will feast well tonight
bones snapping, fur and skin tearing

sweet meats, sweet blood, no sharing
those rapid heartbeats a tempting song
bones snapping, fur and skin tearing
the call of prey is so strong

exile

Fox found
her family
they made it clear she was
a threat. not mother. not mate. but
monster

rest

Fox dreamt in her ice cave den
her frayed white coat kept her warm by a thread
it felt good to be out in the wide open
the metal prison no longer her bed

her frayed white coat kept her warm by a thread
the fool searched in vain
the metal prison no longer her bed
Fox would see him again

the fool searched in vain
she thought of the caged beasts she'd avenge
Fox would see him again
readying to exact her revenge

she thought of the caged beasts she'd avenge
it felt good to be out in the wide open
readying to exact her revenge
Fox dreamt in her ice cave den

Part IV
marriage in the making

the location

mendenhall
gorgeous venue
a stunning blue glacial hall
a compelling ingenue

gorgeous venue
an intimate setting
a compelling ingenue
but why was Roen fretting?

an intimate setting
celebrating with family and friends
but why was Roen fretting?
its icy beauty transcends

celebrating with family and friends
a stunning blue glacial hall
its icy beauty transcends
mendenhall

stranger danger

Fox hears
a familiar
voice, a violation
of solitude that awakens
her rage

setting the stage

it's perfect—it will be a breeze
you'll enter by dogsled
the planner put them at ease
they look forward to being newly wed

you'll enter by dogsled
they agree to take pictures at the ice cave
they look forward to being newly wed
a perfect location for their grave

they agree to take pictures at the ice cave
note the blues, greens, and hints of indigo
a perfect location for their grave
Fox watches them from the banks of snow

note the blues, greens, and hints of indigo
the planner put them at ease
Fox watches them from the banks of snow
it's perfect—it will be a breeze

save the date

they would come
from near and far
her father, his mum
a friend with her guitar

from near and far
his uncle, her aunt
a friend with her guitar
they were up for the jaunt

his uncle, her aunt
friends from the lab
they were up for the jaunt
the more to grab

friends from the lab
her father, his mum
the more to grab
they would come

something old

Papa
gave her momma's
sequined wedding dress, a
way for Momma to stand with her
that day

something new

his mum
presented him
with a set of cufflinks
Grandfather's sigil engraved, two
mountains

something red

lacy
ruby red and
delicate, she held the
lingerie against her skin and
shuddered

something's askew

Roen
caught something in
the corner of his eye
a flash of something familiar
savage

premonition

in her dream but not a dream
there was a creature by Octavia's bed
in the dark, its snarl formed a scream
its eyes gleaming a bloody red

there was a creature by Octavia's bed
a thousand-tooth smile took over its face
its eyes gleaming a bloody red
her heart started to race

a thousand-tooth smile took over its face
its claws positioned over her throat
her heart started to race
she croaked a desperate, pleading note

its claws positioned over her throat
in the dark, its snarl formed a scream
she croaked a desperate, pleading note
was it a dream, or not a dream?

honeymoon plans

cagey
that's how they felt
it would do them some good
to frolic in warm climates and
escape

rehearsal dinner

fear was a delicious meal of dreams
the wedding party sipped wine
Fox feasted on muffled screams
the food and laughter were divine

the wedding party sipped wine
the poor fellow didn't have a chance
the food and laughter were divine
Fox tore at the man in a hungry trance

the poor fellow didn't have a chance
has anyone seen Ted?
Fox tore at the man in a hungry trance
jet lag—he's probably in bed

has anyone seen Ted?
Fox feasted on muffled screams
jet lag—he's probably in bed
fear was a delicious meal of dreams

in memoriam

we carry them with us
their ghosts
they sat in a moment of silence
our hearts serve as hosts

their ghosts
with Grandfather and Momma
our hearts serve as hosts
Fox's sisters and brethren in trauma

with Grandfather and Momma
we feel the pain of their absence
Fox's sisters and brethren in trauma
gone but never forgotten

we feel the pain of their absence
they sat in a moment of silence
gone but never forgotten
we carry them with us

kiss me good night

kiss me good night
Octavia reached for Roen
it's our last night
happy lives to be overthrown

Octavia reached for Roen
Fox watched them from the dark
happy lives to be overthrown
tomorrow would be tragic and stark

Fox watched them from the dark
her lips soft and tender
tomorrow would be tragic and stark
their heartbeats an intoxicating splendor

her lips soft and tender
it's our last night
their heartbeats an intoxicating splendor
kiss me good night

Part V
'til death parts us

flowers for the bride

she chose
dahlias for
love eternal, roses
for passion, and yarrow for her
momma

pocket bouquet

when he
opened the small
box and extracted the
buttercup boutonniere, he smiled
my girl

superstitious

you're not supposed to see me in my dress! go away!
Roen wrapped his arms around Octavia's waist
Fox watched her prey
waiting for her first taste

Roen wrapped his arms around Octavia's waist
she laughed when he nibbled her ear
waiting for her first taste
Fox huddled near

she laughed when he nibbled her ear
i'm serious! it's bad luck, my dear!
Fox huddled near
then made her way to the glacier

i'm serious! it's bad luck, my dear!
Fox watched her prey
then made her way to the glacier
you'll never see your bride after today

minus one

groomsmen
looked for Ted to
no avail, no luck (Ted
was dead, headless, and dragged to a
dark grave)

ladies in waiting

eager for their arrival
Octavia's girlfriends wore green
they stood by the glacial wall
Fox waited, hidden, unseen

Octavia's girlfriends wore green
shivering in their coats
Fox waited, hidden, unseen
the wedding planner checked her notes

shivering in their coats
Fox stared at them, tempting treats
the wedding planner checked her notes
energized by their heartbeats

Fox stared at them, tempting treats
they stood by the glacial wall
energized by their heartbeats
eager for their arrival

a race to the first

race you!
two dogsleds at
the ready, bride and groom
get in their sleds, jockeying to
be first

hesitant

the dogs
mushing ahead
detected a danger
in the air, a warning to halt
go back

first look photos

some pictures tell the story of a lifetime
other photos would become ephemera
smile for the camera!
the wedding party laughed and made faces

other photos would become ephemera
the photographer had a sharp eye
the wedding party laughed and made faces
did she see something white flash by?

the photographer had a sharp eye
distracted by guests' applause
did she see something white flash by?
the blurred image gave her pause

distracted by guests' applause
smile for the camera!
the blurred image gave her pause
some pictures tell the story of a lifetime

ceremony

we gather here to bear witness
they took each other's hands
Octavia looked resplendent in her dress
Fox emerged from the snowy bands

they took each other's hands
to celebrate this union
Fox emerged from the snowy bands
Octavia and Roen

to celebrate this union
Fox barreled toward them
Octavia and Roen
Fox's teeth bore down on the groom

Fox barreled toward them
Octavia looked resplendent in her dress
Fox's teeth bore down on the groom
they did not want to bear witness

thunderstruck ii

Roen was thunderstruck by it
how did Fox move so quickly?
he had no choice but to submit
Fox tore into his femoral artery

how did Fox move so quickly?
guests screamed, an unnerving thrum
Fox tore into his femoral artery
he felt his body go numb

guests screamed, an unnerving thrum
his blood flowed and quivered
he felt his body go numb
Fox's revenge delivered

his blood flowed and quivered
he had no choice but to submit
Fox's revenge delivered
Roen was thunderstruck by it

woman scorned

Octavia wished the screaming would stop
it was her scream, bloody and tinged
she could hear her eardrums pop
she was a woman unhinged

it was her scream, bloody and tinged
Octavia raced to Roen
she was a woman unhinged
Fox relished Roen's death moan

Octavia raced to Roen
ignoring the danger ahead
Fox relished Roen's death moan
but it was Fox's turn to feel dread

ignoring the danger ahead
she could hear her eardrums pop
but it was Fox's turn to feel dread
Octavia screamed and wouldn't stop

bubbly

she grabbed
the first thing she
saw, a makeshift weapon
and ran, clawed, and slipped on the ice
and blood

she smashed
the large champagne
bottle against Fox's head
when it broke, she took a shard to
Fox's throat

Fox tried
to escape her
but Fox had become prey
Octavia unleashed her rage
and pain

Fox could
feel her life fade
the woman's ivory
sequined dress and Fox's white coat drenched
in death

crimson vows

their desire to wed remains unchanged
Octavia tears her momma's dress
crimson vows exchanged
she tries to stop the bloody mess

Octavia tears her momma's dress
Roen gives her the rings
she tries to stop the bloody mess
to have and to hold one last time stings

Roen gives her the rings
chaplain delivers marital blessings and last rites
to have and to hold one last time stings
'til death parts us

chaplain delivers marital blessings and last rites
crimson vows exchanged
'til death parts us
their desire to wed remains unchanged

seven minutes

in their last minutes
he dreamt of dancing with Octavia
they found peace within death's limits
pounce, pounce, pounce

he dreamt of dancing with Octavia
paramedics are here—stay with me
pounce, pounce, pounce
Fox imagined hunting with her family

paramedics are here—stay with me
goodbye, Octavia, my love
Fox imagined hunting with her family
Roen saw Octavia cradle his body from above

goodbye, Octavia, my love
they found peace within death's limits
Roen saw Octavia cradle his body from above
in their last minutes

procession

humans
took Fox from her
kit, and did things to her
that scared them. they watched the woman
kill Fox

humans
left Fox on the
glacier, dead and drenched in
blood. her kit saw not *monster*, but
Momma

they nudged
her; she did not
stir. they took Fox to her
ice cave. they would not forgive or
forget

shattered

they thought
they would grow old
a fantasy marred by
testing nature, their forever
shattered

reception

Octavia transformed into widow and wife
in a single day
she entered in sequins and strife
holding her bouquet

in a single day
surrounded by so much sorrow
holding her bouquet
there wasn't enough yarrow

surrounded by so much sorrow
the shock made her body quake
there wasn't enough yarrow
Momma's flowers could not fix her heartbreak

the shock made her body quake
she entered in sequins and strife
Momma's flowers could not fix her heartbreak
Octavia transformed into widow and wife

eulogy

you were with me but a lifetime ago
we were joyful standing here
there will never be a tomorrow
with you, no happy new year

we were joyful standing here
now i stand weeping by your grave
with you, no happy new year
i'm struggling to be brave

now i stand weeping by your grave
a place no flowers grow
i'm struggling to be brave
my love, i miss you so

a place no flowers grow
there will never be a tomorrow
my love, i miss you so
you were with me but a lifetime ago

haunted widow/haunted life

all houses are haunted
where people lived and died
Longfellow's poem taunted
Octavia entered their home and cried

where people lived and died
that's where she resided
Octavia entered their home and cried
where Roen's ghost presided

that's where she resided
at their home, at his grave
where Roen's ghost presided
she felt neither comforted nor brave

at their home, at his grave
Longfellow's poem taunted
she felt neither comforted nor brave
all houses to her are haunted

Epilogue

three years later

her antidote
all those years ago
Octavia found notes she wrote
helping troubled crops and flowers grow

all those years ago
when she was happy
helping troubled crops and flowers grow
when she was inquisitive and scrappy

when she was happy
the sad fog lifted a bit
when she was inquisitive and scrappy
maybe this was it

the sad fog lifted a bit
Octavia found notes she wrote
maybe this was it
her antidote

Octavia's folly

she watched her experiment unfold
Octavia grew yarrow and buttercups
a sea of white and gold
broken heart pick-me-ups

Octavia grew yarrow and buttercups
a remembrance of his charm
broken heart pick-me-ups
but something caused her alarm

a remembrance of his charm
at the gravesite of her beau
but something caused her alarm
flashes of white and indigo

at the gravesite of her beau
a sea of white and gold
flashes of white and indigo
she watched her experiment unfold

reunited

they were together once again
she was no longer Grief's slave
Octavia embraced Roen
locals found her bloodied body by his grave

she was no longer Grief's slave
Octavia saw him holding a buttercup
locals found her bloodied body by his grave
Roen smiled at her gardening getup

Octavia saw him holding a buttercup
hello, my love
Roen smiled at her gardening getup
hello, beautiful

hello, my love
Octavia embraced Roen
hello, beautiful
they were together once again

whispers of the vale

if you
wed in the spot
known as Crimson Vows Vale
bring yarrow and buttercups for
good luck

if you
wed in the spot
known as Crimson Vows Vale
and see indigo flecks, death will
part you

acknowledgments

To the incomparable poet and editor, Shelby Leigh, I am grateful for your guidance, empathy, and suggestions during the developmental editing stages. To Ground Crew Editorial's Ariane Peveto and Jackie Peveto, thank you for your eagle-eyed copyediting, for embracing the wonder of this story, and for your guidance on how to classify this work. Thank you to Islam Farid for adding to the atmosphere of the book with your book cover design.

Thank you to R. B. Wood and The House of Gamut. If I had not joined this community, I may have never read *Numinous Stones* by Holly Lyn Walrath and fallen in love with the pantoum poem format she uses in her book.

I am forever grateful to friends Tami Osborne, Lauren Palmer, Julie Shaw, and Eileen Walsh for reading early versions and cheering me on to the finish line.

Finally, I'd like to thank my husband, Tito. This book is based on a short story I wrote a few years ago. He was the first to encourage me to expand it into a book. Thank you, my lovely weirdo. xo

about the poem formats

I wrote this book using two types of poem formats, pantoum and cinquain.

The pantoum is a poem of any length, composed of four-line stanzas in which the second and fourth lines of each stanza serve as the first and third lines of the next stanza. The last line of a pantoum is often the same as the first. The pantoum originated in Malaysia in the fifteenth-century as a short folk poem, typically made up of two rhyming couplets that were recited or sung. (Information source: https://poets.org/glossary/pantoum)

The cinquain, also known as a quintain or quintet, is a poem or stanza composed of five lines. Examples of cinquains can be found in many European languages, and the origin of the form dates back to medieval French poetry. The most common cinquains in English follow a rhyme scheme of *ababb*, *abaab* or *abccb*. (Information source: https://poets.org/glossary/cinquain)

about the author

Cheryl Cantafio is a poetry and children's book writer from Norristown, Pennsylvania. When she's not writing, she works in information technology, co-hosts a podcast (*You Only Go Once*), reads gothic horror or thriller novels, or binge-watches movies and television series. Her book *My Stay with the Sisters: Poems* was her debut as an author and poet in May 2023. *Barry and the Big Jump* will be her debut children's book, set to release in November 2024.

Connect with her on Instagram: @cherylc.writer

about the editors and book cover designer

Shelby Leigh is the bestselling poet of *changing with the tides* and *girl made of glass*. Passionate about helping others feel less alone through poetry, her newest book *from sand to stars* (Central Avenue Publishing) explores time and how it affects our mental health. Leigh is proud to support the poetry community and encourage others to find their voice through poetry editing and workshops. Connect with Shelby at shelbyleigh.co and on Instagram at @shelbyleighpoetry.

Jackie Peveto is a writer, artist, reader, and enthusiast for anything else involving imagination and paper. She has a master's degree in creative writing and studied in Japan and at the University of Oxford, where she read as many books as she could. Her work has been published in *The Garbanzo Literary Journal*, *YARN*, and *Kite Tales*, and she currently runs a small editorial business with her twin sister.

Ariane Peveto is a writer and editor who enjoys helping others bring their stories and ideas to life. She started out as a writing tutor and then taught courses in composition and rhetoric for college students. After making the very natural step from there to become an editor, Ariane had the privilege of working on a wide variety of projects, like one of NYT bestselling author Dave Asprey's books and a text for Biola University—as well as dozens of independent clients with everything from picture books to memoir, young adult novels to adult sci-fi. She currently runs a small editorial business with her twin sister.

Islam Farid is a freelancer graphic designer specializing in editorial design and cover art. He has been working in design for over ten years. Islam currently works with individual authors and publishing houses worldwide. He creates unique and distinctive imagery for both fiction and nonfiction publications.

Connect with Islam at islamfarid.net

Printed in the USA
CPSIA information can be obtained
at www.ICGtesting.com
CBHW060503280824
13785CB00014B/332